Cambridge Early Years

Let's Explore

Learner's Book 3C

Kathryn Harper & Philippa Hines

Contents

Note to parents and practitioners — 3

Block 5: How things work — 4

Block 6: Space and the future — 18

Acknowledgements — 32

Note to parents and practitioners

This Learner's Book provides activities to support the third term of Let's Explore for Cambridge Early Years 3.

Activities can be used at school or at home. Children will need support from an adult. Additional guidance about activities can be found in the **For practitioners** boxes.

Some activities use stickers. The stickers can be found in the section in the middle of this book.

Stories are provided for children to enjoy looking at and listening to. Children are not expected to be able to read the stories themselves.

Children will encounter the following characters within this book. You could ask children to point to the characters when they see them on the pages, and say their names.

The Learner's Book activities support the Teaching Resource activities. The Teaching Resource provides step-by-step coverage of the Cambridge Early Years curriculum and guidance on how the Learner's Book activities develop the curriculum learning statements.

Hi, my name is Mia.

Find us on the front covers doing lots of fun activities.

Hi, my name is Gemi.

Hi, my name is Rafi.

Hi, my name is Kiho.

Block 5 How things work

Forces in the park
Choose stickers and say.

For practitioners

Children explore the picture and discuss what they can see. Children stick the matching pictures in place, e.g., paper flowers to craft tent. Explore the picture together and ask *What forces are being used?* Encourage children to find Rafi in the picture.

Push and pull
Match.

For practitioners
Review the meaning of the words *push* and *pull* with children and then ask them to describe the pictures. Draw a line to match together the actions showing the push forces and the actions showing the pull forces.

Slide or roll
Draw and say.

For practitioners
Talk about what makes items slide or roll, e.g., a smooth flat surface or wheels. Children draw a toy from their classroom that they think will slide or roll. Discuss drawings as a group, encouraging children to offer explanations for their thinking. Ask *How can we make the object move? Will it roll or slide? Do you need to push it or pull it?* They could test this out with the toy.

Rolling
Draw.

How do you like to roll?

For practitioners
Children draw a picture of them doing something that involves rolling, such as playing with a ball, being in a car, riding a scooter or bike, or rolling on the grass or down a hill. How does it feel to ride over bumps or roll on the ground? Does it feel like pushing or pulling? Ask children to share their experiences.

Which material are these made from?
Stick and say.

plastic

wood

metal

For practitioners
Talk about the three materials with children and show some examples of items made from each material. Children stick the stickers in the correct category. Then they say what the materials are.

metal

paper

fabric

Magnetic or not magnetic?

Join the dots and match.

For practitioners
Children join the dots to complete the pictures. Talk about how magnets are attracted to metal objects. You may need to remind them what the word *magnetic* means. Ask *Can you describe what happens when magnets touch different materials? Which of the objects on this page do you think are magnetic?*

Clay pots
Think, cut and paste.

For practitioners

Using magazines, fabrics, card and any other craft materials you have available in your setting, children design a clay pot by cutting and pasting materials. Encourage them to discuss their pots with their peers as they design it, offering suggestions or following others' ideas to incorporate into their own designs: *Do you like the colour of Isha's pot? Is there a nice pattern on Hafiz's pot, Ismail?*

Papier mâché

Think, draw and stick.

For practitioners
Talk about what things are made of papier mâché (you may need to give suggestions or show pictures of things). Ask *If you could create anything, what would you make using papier mâché?* Children then draw these imaginary creations in the space provided. They can also add to their drawings by gluing coloured paper or pieces of tissue paper to it. Encourage children to talk about their drawings with a partner and explain why they have chosen to use certain colours or patterns.

Which one is electric?
Say and circle.

For practitioners
Look at the pictures of the instruments. Ask *What makes an instrument electronic?*
Talk about how each instrument is played and what is needed for it to make a sound.
Children circle the ones that are electronic and demonstrate or say what kind of sound it makes.

Stickers for pages 4–5

Stickers for pages 18–19

Stickers for page 9

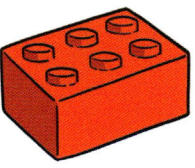

Simon Says
Write.

For practitioners
Talk about the game 'Simon Says', reminding children how to play it if they have forgotten. Children then pick their own action words to do as part of the game, which they then write in a speech bubble. They can write four each to fill the bubbles. Children then play the game in pairs, giving their partner the instructions to follow in the style of the game, for example *Simon Says touch your nose*. Encourage children to take turns and to swap partners.

Block 6 Space and the future

What can you see in space?
Choose stickers and say.

For practitioners
Children explore the picture and discuss what they can see. Children stick the matching pictures in place, e.g., astronaut to spacecraft. Explore the picture together and ask *What planets can you see?* Encourage children to find Mia in the picture.

Why is the sun important?
Read and draw.

The sun gives us light.

The sun helps plants grow.

The sun gives us energy.

For practitioners
Talk about why the sun is important in our lives. Look at each picture and discuss how the sun is helping. Encourage children to notice that the sun is a source of heat and light. Children then draw a picture of something they like to do in the sun.

Help the astronaut get home
Draw.

For practitioners
Children draw a line to return the astronaut to Earth. Along the way, children should identify the different things they see. Encourage children to name the different planets if they know them but it is not essential. Ask *Which planets do you know? Where do we live?*

Space Adventure!
Read and say.

For practitioners

Read the story and ask children to imagine the sounds and voices of the characters. Point out how sometimes the sound is shown in the pictures. Then read again and let children create the sounds. They can then do movements to match the sound effects in the story.

Space Adventure! character

Draw and write.

My character's name is: _____

What do they like to do? _____

How do they talk? _____

How do they move? _____

For practitioners

Children choose a character from the *Space Adventure!* story or make up a new one and draw it. Then they think about their personality and answer the questions. Encourage children to use their imaginations here as the story was short and we didn't learn much about the characters. Children can then role-play their creation in small groups.

Space comic
Draw and write.

1.

2.

3

4

For practitioners
Children draw a sequence of events to tell a story. Talk about their ideas before they start. Ask children to suggest ideas perhaps from stories or films they know. Model this by suggesting one of your own ideas and what you would draw in each of the boxes. Children draw and then share their stories in pairs or small groups.

Pictures of you!

Draw and say.

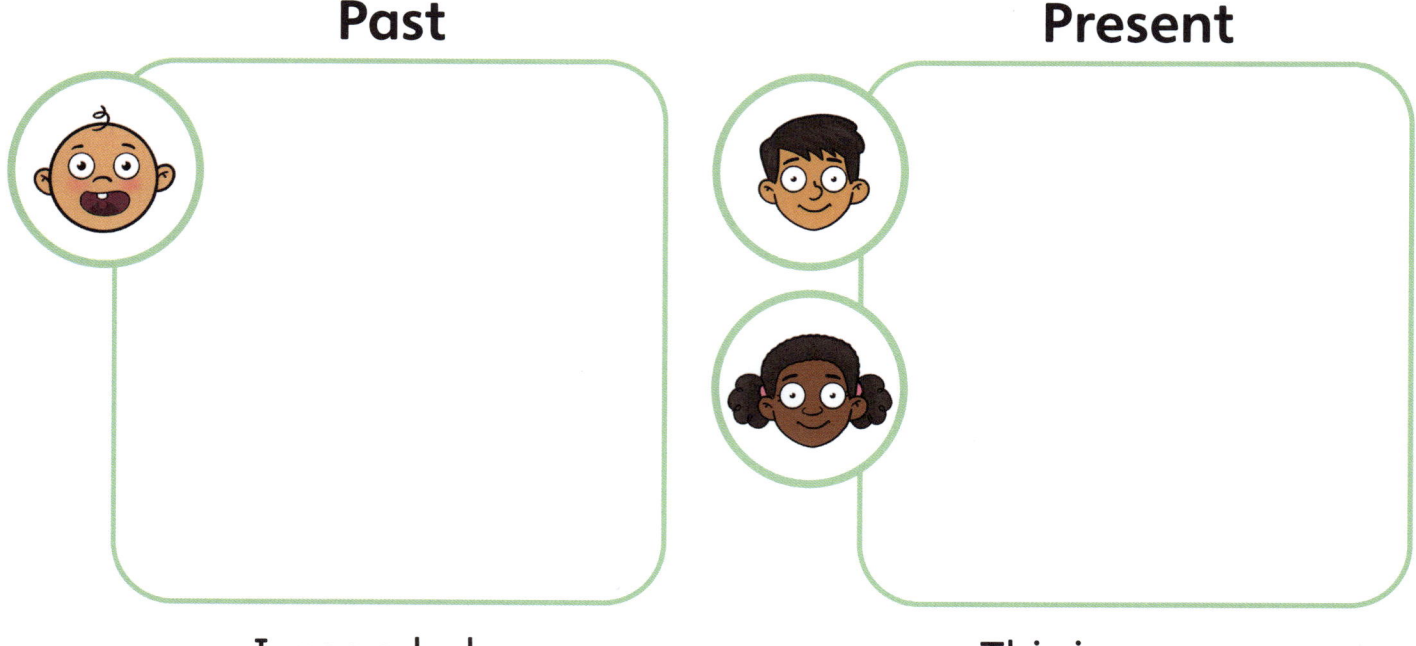

Past

I was a baby.

Present

This is me now.

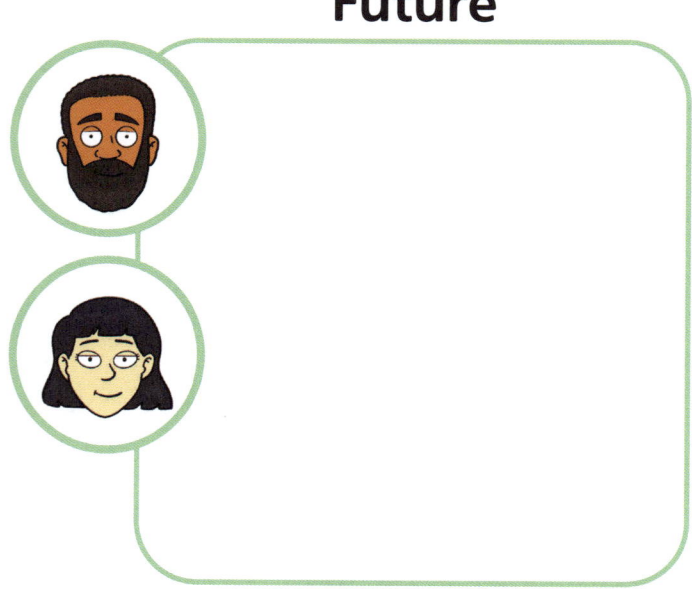

Future

I will be an adult.

For practitioners
Remind children of the words *past*, *present* and *future*. Children draw pictures of themselves doing something that they did when they were a baby, that they can do now and that they will do when they are an adult. Encourage children to talk about things that they did in the past, do in the present and will do in the future.

What do they do?

Match and name.

- You pay for your shopping here.
- You listen with these.
- You walk through these.
- You type words with this.
- You take pictures with this.

For practitioners
Children match the pictures to the description of how they're used. Ask them to name and talk about the items (automatic doors, camera, headphones, keyboard, self checkout).

Community jobs
Act and play.

Start ▶ Move 3 spaces. ▶ Move 2 spaces.

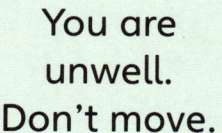
You are unwell. Don't move.

Move 2 spaces.

Move 1 space.

Move 2 spaces.

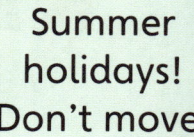
Summer holidays! Don't move.

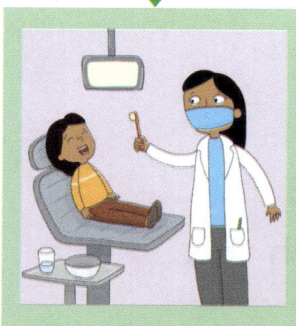
Move 2 spaces.

Move 3 spaces.

Move 1 space.

Move 2 spaces.

Move 2 spaces.

For practitioners
Children roll a dice or use a spinner to play the game. When they arrive on a square, they must act out the job shown. Then they can move forward as indicated. If they don't land on a job, they must stay in place until their next turn. The first player to reach the end wins.

Break time! Don't move.

Move 2 spaces.

Move 3 spaces.

Lunchtime. Don't move.

Move 2 spaces.

Move 1 space.

Move 3 spaces.

Move 2 spaces.

Bedtime. Don't move.

Move 1 space.

New Year's holiday. Don't move.

Move 1 space.

Move 1 space.

Move 2 spaces.

Move 1 space.

You win!

Move 1 space.

Move 2 spaces.

Move 3 spaces.

There's a big storm. Don't move.

What do you think about big school?

Read and circle.

		😊	😐	☹️
1	I have seen my new school.	😊	😐	☹️
2	I know my new teacher.	😊	😐	☹️
3	My friends are going to my new school.	😊	😐	☹️
4	I will do a lot of activities at my new school.	😊	😐	☹️
5	I will have a uniform at my new school.	😊	😐	☹️
6	I will learn a lot at my new school.	😊	😐	☹️

For practitioners

Read each sentence together and ask children to circle how they feel. For each sentence, encourage children to discuss why they feel happy, sad or don't know. For example, if they don't know or are sad, discuss and encourage children to suggest ways in which they can begin to think positively about their new school. Remind them of when they started this school and how they became comfortable and happy here.

How was your school year?

Read and tick.

I can remember lots of things from school this year.

I can remember:

- ☐ my favourite song
- ☐ my favourite game
- ☐ my favourite story
- ☐ my favourite toy
- ☐ my favourite activity

For practitioners
Explain that there are no right or wrong answers. Read and talk about the sentences. Ask *What can you remember?* For each sentence, encourage children to discuss their answers, sharing their favourite songs, stories, etc. with a partner. Encourage children to feel positive about their achievements.

Acknowledgements

The authors and publishers acknowledge the following sources of copyright material and are grateful for the permissions granted. While every effort has been made, it has not always been possible to identify the sources of all the material used, or to trace all copyright holders. If any omissions are brought to our notice, we will be happy to include the appropriate acknowledgements on reprinting.

Thanks to the following for permission to reproduce images:

p9 Stockbyte/GI, sakdam/GI, Firmafotografen/GI; p10 Rawpixel/GI; p16 JUN2/GI, Suradech14/GI, porpeller/GI, Yevgen Romanenko/GI, nikkytok/GI, imagenavi/GI; p17 Jose Luis Pelaez/GI; p20 CR/GI, khoa vu/GI, querbeet/GI; p27 AlesVeluscek/GI, wir0man/GI, Issarawat Tattong/GI, Yaorusheng/GI, ozanuysal/GI

Thanks to the following artists at Beehive Illustration:

Laura Arias, Helen Graper, Michelle McGovern, Claire Philpott, Joe Wilkins.

Cover characters by Becky Davies (The Bright Agency)